A WODEHOUSE *Pick-Me-Up!*

The Amazing Hat Mystery

arrow books

3 5 7 9 10 8 6 4 2

Arrow Books
20 Vauxhall Bridge Road
London SW1V 2SA

Arrow Books is part of the Penguin Random House group of companies
whose addresses can be found at global.penguinrandomhouse.com

Penguin
Random House
UK

All stories from *Young Men in Spats*, first published in the United Kingdom
by Herbert Jenkins Ltd in 1936; published by Arrow Books in 2008
This collection first published in the United Kingdom by Arrow Books in 2017

www.penguin.co.uk

www.wodehouse.co.uk

A CIP catalogue record for this book is available from the British Library.

ISBN 9781787460126

Typeset in 12/14 pt Perpetua Std by Jouve (UK), Milton Keynes
Printed and bound in Great Britain by Clays Ltd, Elcograf S.p.A.

MIX
Paper from
responsible sources
FSC www.fsc.org FSC® C018179

Penguin Random House is committed to a
sustainable future for our business, our readers
and our planet. This book is made from Forest
Stewardship Council® certified paper.

CONTENTS

THE AMAZING HAT MYSTERY

A bean was in a nursing-home with a broken leg as the result of trying to drive his sports-model Poppenheim through the Marble Arch instead of round it, and a kindly Crumpet had looked in to give him the gossip of the town. He found him playing halma with the nurse, and he sat down on the bed and took a grape, and the Bean asked what was going on in the great world.

'Well,' said the Crumpet, taking another grape, 'the finest minds in the Drones are still wrestling with the great Hat mystery.'

'What's that?'

'You don't mean you haven't heard about it?'

'Not a word.'

The Crumpet was astounded. He swallowed two grapes at once in his surprise.

'Why, London's seething with it. The general consensus of opinion is that it has something to do with the Fourth Dimension. You know how things go. I mean to say, something rummy occurs and you consult some big-brained bird and he wags his head and says "Ah! The Fourth Dimension!" Extraordinary nobody's told you about the great Hat mystery.'

'You're the first visitor I've had. What is it, anyway? What hat?'

'Well, there were two hats. Reading from left to right, Percy Wimbolt's and Nelson Cork's.'

The Bean nodded intelligently.

'I see what you mean. Percy had one, and Nelson had the other.'

'Exactly. Two hats in all. Top hats.'

'What was mysterious about them?'

'Why, Elizabeth Bottsworth and Diana Punter said they didn't fit.'

'Well, hats don't sometimes.'

'But these came from Bodmin's.'

The Bean shot up in bed. 'What?'

'You mustn't excite the patient,' said the nurse, who up to this point had taken no part in the conversation.

'But, dash it, nurse,' cried the Bean, 'you can't have caught what he said. If we are to give credence to his story, Percy Wimbolt and Nelson Cork bought a couple of hats at Bodmin's — at *Bodmin's*, I'll trouble you — and they didn't fit. It isn't possible.'

He spoke with strong emotion, and the Crumpet nodded understandingly. People can say what they please about the modern young man believing in nothing nowadays, but there is one thing every right-minded young man believes in, and that is the infallibility of Bodmin's hats. It is one of the eternal verities. Once admit that it is possible for a Bodmin hat not to fit, and you leave the door open for Doubt, Schism, and Chaos generally.

'That's exactly how Percy and Nelson felt, and it was for that reason that they were compelled to take the strong line they did with E. Bottsworth and D. Punter.'

'They took a strong line, did they?'

'A very strong line.'

'Won't you tell us the whole story from the beginning?' said the nurse.

'Right ho,' said the Crumpet, taking a grape. 'It'll make your head swim.'

'So mysterious?'

'So absolutely dashed uncanny from start to finish.'

You must know, to begin with, my dear old nurse (said the Crumpet), that these two blokes, Percy Wimbolt and Nelson Cork, are fellows who have to exercise the most watchful care about their lids, because they are so situated that in their case there can be none of that business of just charging into any old hattery and grabbing the first thing in sight. Percy is one of those large, stout, outsize chaps with a head like a water-melon, while Nelson is built more on the lines of a minor jockey and has a head like a peanut.

You will readily appreciate, therefore, that it requires an artist hand to fit them properly and that is why they have always gone to Bodmin. I have heard Percy say that his trust in Bodmin is like the unspotted faith of a young

3

curate in his Bishop and I have no doubt that Nelson would have said the same, if he had thought of it.

It was at Bodmin's door that they ran into each other on the morning when my story begins.

'Hullo,' said Percy. 'You come to buy a hat?'

'Yes,' said Nelson. 'You come to buy a hat?'

'Yes.' Percy glanced cautiously about him, saw that he was alone (except for Nelson, of course) and unobserved, and drew closer and lowered his voice. 'There's a reason!'

'That's rummy,' said Nelson. He, also, spoke in a hushed tone. 'I have a special reason, too.'

Percy looked warily about, and lowered his voice another notch.

'Nelson,' he said, 'you know Elizabeth Bottsworth?'

'Intimately,' said Nelson.

'Rather a sound young potato, what?'

'Very much so.'

'Pretty.'

'I've often noticed it.'

'Me, too. She is so small, so sweet, so dainty, so lively, so viv— what's-the-word? – that a fellow wouldn't be far out in calling her an angel in human shape.'

'Aren't all angels in human shape?'

'Are they?' said Percy, who was a bit foggy on angels. 'Well, be that as it may,' he went on, his cheeks suffused to a certain extent, 'I love that girl, Nelson, and she's coming with me to the first day of Ascot, and I'm relying on this new hat of mine to do just that extra bit that's needed in the way of making her reciprocate my passion. Having only met her so far at country-houses, I've never yet flashed upon her in a topper.'

Nelson Cork was staring.

'Well, if that isn't the most remarkable coincidence I ever came across in my puff!' he exclaimed, amazed. 'I'm buying my new hat for exactly the same reason.'

A convulsive start shook Percy's massive frame. His eyes bulged.

'To fascinate Elizabeth Bottsworth?' he cried, beginning to writhe.

'No, no,' said Nelson, soothingly. 'Of course not. Elizabeth and I have always been great friends, but nothing more. What I meant was that I, like you, am counting on this forthcoming topper of mine to put me across with the girl I love.'

Percy stopped writhing.

'Who is she?' he asked, interested.

'Diana Punter, the niece of my godmother, old Ma Punter. It's an odd thing, I've known her all my life – brought up as kids together and so forth – but it's only recently that passion has burgeoned. I now worship that girl, Percy, from the top of her head to the soles of her divine feet.'

Percy looked dubious.

'That's a pretty longish distance, isn't it? Diana Punter is one of my closest friends, and a charming girl in every respect, but isn't she a bit tall for you, old man?'

'My dear chap, that's just what I admire so much

about her, her superb statuesqueness. More like a Greek goddess than anything I've struck for years. Besides, she isn't any taller for me than you are for Elizabeth Bottsworth.'

'True,' admitted Percy.

'And, anyway, I love her, blast it, and I don't propose to argue the point. I love her, I love her, I love her, and we are lunching together the first day of Ascot.'

'At Ascot?'

'No. She isn't keen on racing, so I shall have to give Ascot a miss.'

'That's Love,' said Percy, awed.

'The binge will take place at my godmother's house in Berkeley Square, and it won't be long after that, I feel, before you see an interesting announcement in the *Morning Post*.'

Percy extended his hand. Nelson grasped it warmly.

'These new hats are pretty well bound to do the trick, I should say, wouldn't you?'

'Infallibly. Where girls are concerned, there is nothing that brings home the gravy like a well-fitting topper.'

'Bodmin must extend himself as never before,' said Percy.

'He certainly must,' said Nelson.

They entered the shop. And Bodmin, having measured them with his own hands, promised that two of his very finest efforts should be at their respective addresses in the course of the next few days.

*

Now, Percy Wimbolt isn't a chap you would suspect of having nerves, but there is no doubt that in the interval which elapsed before Bodmin was scheduled to deliver he got pretty twittery. He kept having awful visions of some great disaster happening to his new hat: and, as things turned out, these visions came jolly near being fulfilled. It has made Percy feel that he is psychic.

What occurred was this. Owing to these jitters of his, he hadn't been sleeping any too well, and on the morning before Ascot he was up as early as ten-thirty, and he went to his sitting-room window to see what sort of a day it was, and the sight he beheld from that window absolutely froze the blood in his veins.

For there below him, strutting up and down the pavement, were a uniformed little blighter whom he recognized as Bodmin's errand-boy and an equally foul kid in mufti. And balanced on each child's loathsome head was a top hat. Against the railings were leaning a couple of cardboard hat-boxes.

Now, considering that Percy had only just woken from a dream in which he had been standing outside the Guildhall in his new hat, receiving the Freedom of the City from the Lord Mayor, and the Lord Mayor had suddenly taken a terrific swipe at the hat with his mace, knocking it into hash, you might have supposed that he would have been hardened to anything. But he wasn't. His reaction was terrific. There was a moment of sort of paralysis, during which he was telling himself that he had always suspected this beastly little boy of

Bodmin's of having a low and frivolous outlook and being temperamentally unfitted for his high office: and then he came alive with a jerk and let out probably the juiciest yell the neighbourhood had heard for years.

It stopped the striplings like a high-powered shell. One moment, they had been swanking up and down in a mincing and affected sort of way: the next, the second kid had legged it like a streak and Bodmin's boy was shoving the hats back in the boxes and trying to do it quickly enough to enable him to be elsewhere when Percy should arrive.

And in this he was successful. By the time Percy had got to the front door and opened it, there was nothing to be seen but a hat-box standing on the steps. He took it up to his flat and removed the contents with a gingerly and reverent hand, holding his breath for fear the nap should have got rubbed the wrong way or a dent of any nature been made in the gleaming surface; but apparently all was well. Bodmin's boy might sink to taking hats out of their boxes and fooling about with them, but at least he hadn't gone to the last awful extreme of dropping them.

The lid was O.K. absolutely: and on the following morning Percy, having spent the interval polishing it with stout, assembled the boots, the spats, the trousers, the coat, the flowered waistcoat, the collar, the shirt, the quiet grey tie, and the good old gardenia, and set off in a taxi for the house where Elizabeth was staying. And presently he was ringing the bell and being told she would be down in a minute, and eventually down she came, looking perfectly marvellous.

'What ho, what ho!' said Percy.

'Hullo, Percy,' said Elizabeth.

Now, naturally, up to this moment Percy had been standing with bared head. At this point, he put the hat on. He wanted her to get the full effect suddenly in a good light. And very strategic, too. I mean to say, it would have been the act of a juggins to have waited till they were in the taxi, because in a taxi all toppers look much alike.

So Percy popped the hat on his head with a meaning glance and stood waiting for the uncontrollable round of applause.

And instead of clapping her little hands in girlish ecstasy and doing Spring dances round him, this young Bottsworth gave a sort of gurgling scream not unlike a coloratura soprano choking on a fish-bone.

Then she blinked and became calmer.

'It's all right,' she said. 'The momentary weakness has passed. Tell me, Percy, when do you open?'

'Open?' said Percy, not having the remotest.

'On the Halls. Aren't you going to sing comic songs on the Music Halls?'

Percy's perplexity deepened.

'Me? No. How? Why? What do you mean?'

'I thought that hat must be part of the make-up and that you were trying it on the dog. I couldn't think of any other reason why you should wear one six sizes too small.'

Percy gasped. 'You aren't suggesting this hat doesn't fit me?'

'It doesn't fit you by a mile.'

'But it's a Bodmin.'

'Call it that if you like. I call it a public outrage.'

Percy was appalled. I mean, naturally. A nice thing for a chap to give his heart to a girl and then find her talking in this hideous, flippant way of sacred subjects.

Then it occurred to him that, living all the time in the country, she might not have learned to appreciate the holy significance of the name Bodmin.

'Listen,' he said gently. 'Let me explain. This hat was made by Bodmin, the world-famous hatter of Vigo Street. He measured me in person and guaranteed a fit.'

'And I nearly had one.'

'And if Bodmin guarantees that a hat shall fit,' proceeded Percy, trying to fight against a sickening sort of feeling that he had been all wrong about this girl, 'it fits. I mean, saying a Bodmin hat doesn't fit is like saying . . . well, I can't think of anything awful enough.'

'That hat's awful enough. It's like something out of a two-reel comedy. Pure Chas. Chaplin. I know a joke's a joke, Percy, and I'm as fond of a laugh as anyone, but there is such a thing as cruelty to animals. Imagine the feelings of the horses at Ascot when they see that hat.'

Poets and other literary blokes talk a lot about falling in love at first sight, but it's equally possible to fall out of love just as quickly. One moment, this girl was the be-all and the end-all, as you might say, of Percy Wimbolt's life. The next, she was just a regrettable young blister with whom he wished to hold no further communication. He could stand a good deal from the sex. Insults directed at himself left him unmoved. But he was not prepared to countenance destructive criticism of a Bodmin hat.

'Possibly,' he said, coldly, 'you would prefer to go to this bally race-meeting alone?'

'You bet I'm going alone. You don't suppose I mean to be seen in broad daylight in the paddock at Ascot with a hat like that?'

Percy stepped back and bowed formally.

'Drive on, driver,' he said to the driver, and the driver drove on.

Now, you would say that that was rummy enough. A full-sized mystery in itself, you might call it. But wait. Mark the sequel. You haven't heard anything yet.

We now turn to Nelson Cork. Shortly before one-thirty, Nelson had shoved over to Berkeley Square and had lunch with his godmother and Diana Punter, and Diana's manner and deportment had been absolutely all that could have been desired. In fact, so chummy had she been over the cutlets and fruit salad that it seemed to Nelson that, if she was like this now, imagination boggled at the thought of how utterly all over him she would be when he sprang his new hat on her.

So when the meal was concluded and coffee had

been drunk and old Lady Punter had gone up to her boudoir with a digestive tablet and a sex-novel, he thought it would be a sound move to invite her to come for a stroll along Bond Street. There was the chance, of course, that she would fall into his arms right in the middle of the pavement: but if that happened, he told himself, they could always get into a cab. So he mooted the saunter, and she checked up, and presently they started off.

And you will scarcely believe this, but they hadn't gone more than half-way along Bruton Street when she suddenly stopped and looked at him in an odd manner.

'I don't want to be personal, Nelson,' she said, 'but really I do think you ought to take the trouble to get measured for your hats.'

If a gas main had exploded beneath Nelson's feet, he could hardly have been more taken aback.

'M-m-m-m . . .' he gasped. He could scarcely believe that he had heard aright.

'It's the only way with a head like yours. I know it's a temptation for a lazy man to go into a shop and take just whatever is offered him, but the result is so sloppy. That thing you're wearing now looks like an extinguisher.'

Nelson was telling himself that he must be strong.

'Are you endeavouring to intimate that this hat does not fit?'

'Can't you feel that it doesn't fit?'

'But it's a Bodmin.'

'I don't know what you mean. It's just an ordinary silk hat.'

'Not at all. It's a Bodmin.'

'I don't know what you are talking about.'

'The point I am trying to drive home,' said Nelson, stiffly, 'is that this hat was constructed under the personal auspices of Jno. Bodmin of Vigo Street.'

'Well, it's too big.'

'It is not too big.'

'I say it is too big.'

'And I say a Bodmin hat cannot be too big.'

'Well, I've got eyes, and I say it is.'

Nelson controlled himself with an effort.

'I would be the last person,' he said, 'to criticize your eyesight, but on the present occasion you will permit me to say that it has let you down with a considerable bump. Myopia is indicated. Allow me,' said Nelson, hot under the collar, but still dignified, 'to tell you something about Jno. Bodmin, as the name appears new to you. Jno. is the last of a long line of Bodmins, all of whom have made hats assiduously for the nobility and gentry all their lives. Hats are in Jno. Bodmin's blood.'

'I don't . . .'

Nelson held up a restraining hand.

'Over the door of his emporium in Vigo Street the passers-by may read a significant legend. It runs: "Bespoke Hatter To The Royal Family". That means, in simple language adapted to the lay intelligence, that if the King wants a new topper he simply ankles round to Bodmin's and says: "Good morning, Bodmin, we want a topper." He does not ask if it will fit. He takes it for granted that it will fit. He has bespoken Jno. Bodmin, and he trusts him blindly. You don't suppose His Gracious Majesty would bespeak a hatter whose hats did not fit. The whole essence of being a hatter is to make hats that fit, and it is to this end that Jno. Bodmin has strained every nerve for years. And that is why I say again – simply and without heat – This hat is a Bodmin.'

Diana was beginning to get a bit peeved. The blood of the Punters is hot, and very little is required to steam it up. She tapped Bruton Street with a testy foot.

'You always were an obstinate, pig-headed little fiend, Nelson, even as a child. I tell you once more, for the last time, that that hat is too big. If it were not for the fact that I can see a pair of boots and part of a pair of trousers, I should not know that there was a human being under it. I don't care how much you argue, I still think you ought to be ashamed of yourself for coming out in the thing. Even if you didn't mind for your own sake, you might have considered the feelings of the pedestrians and traffic.'

Nelson quivered.

'You do, do you?'

'Yes, I do.'

'Oh, you do?'

'I said I did. Didn't you hear me? No, I suppose you

could hardly be expected to, with an enormous great hat coming down over your ears.'

'You say this hat comes down over my ears?'

'Right over your ears. It's a mystery to me why you think it worth while to deny it.'

I fear that what follows does not show Nelson Cork in the role of a parfait gentil knight, but in extenuation of his behaviour I must remind you that he and Diana Punter had been brought up as children together, and a dispute between a couple who have shared the same nursery is always liable to degenerate into an exchange of personalities and innuendos. What starts as an academic discussion on hats turns only too swiftly into a raking-up of old sores and a grand parade of family skeletons.

It was so in this case. At the word 'mystery,' Nelson uttered a nasty laugh.

'A mystery, eh? As much a mystery, I suppose, as why your uncle George suddenly left England in the year 1920 without stopping to pack up?'

Diana's eyes flashed. Her foot struck the pavement another shrewd wallop.

'Uncle George,' she said haughtily, 'went abroad for his health.'

'You bet he did,' retorted Nelson. 'He knew what was good for him.'

'Anyway, he wouldn't have worn a hat like that.'

'Where they would have put him if he hadn't been off like a scalded kitten, he wouldn't have worn a hat at all.'

A small groove was now beginning to appear in the paving-stone on which Diana Punter stood.

'Well, Uncle George escaped one thing by going abroad, at any rate,' she said. 'He missed the big scandal about your aunt Clarissa in 1922.'

Nelson clenched his fists. 'The jury gave Aunt Clarissa the benefit of the doubt,' he said hoarsely.

'Well, we all know what that means. It was accompanied, if you recollect, by some very strong remarks from the Bench.'

There was a pause.

'I may be wrong,' said Nelson, 'but I should have thought it ill beseemed a girl whose brother Cyril was warned off the Turf in 1924 to haul up her slacks about other people's Aunt Clarissas.'

'Passing lightly over my brother Cyril in 1924,' rejoined Diana, 'what price your cousin Fred in 1927?'

They glared at one another in silence for a space, each realizing with a pang that the supply of erring relatives had now given out. Diana was still pawing the paving-stone, and Nelson was wondering what on earth he could ever have seen in a girl who, in addition to talking subversive drivel about hats, was eight feet tall and ungainly, to boot.

'While as for your brother-in-law's niece's sister-in-law Muriel . . .' began Diana, suddenly brightening.

Nelson checked her with a gesture.

'I prefer not to continue this discussion,' he said, frigidly.

'It is no pleasure to me,' replied Diana, with equal coldness, 'to have to listen to your vapid gibberings. That's the worst of a man who wears his hat over his mouth – he will talk through it.'

'I bid you a very hearty good afternoon, Miss Punter,' said Nelson.

He strode off without a backward glance.

Now, one advantage of having a row with a girl in Bruton Street is that the Drones is only just round the corner, so that you can pop in and restore the old nervous system with the minimum of trouble. Nelson was round there in what practically amounted to a trice, and the first person he saw was Percy, hunched up over a double and splash.

'Hullo,' said Percy.

'Hullo,' said Nelson.

There was a silence, broken only by the sound of Nelson ordering a mixed vermouth. Percy continued to stare before him like a man who has drained the wine-cup of life to its lees, only to discover a dead mouse at the bottom.

'Nelson,' he said at length, 'what are your views on the Modern Girl?'

'I think she's a mess.'

'I thoroughly agree with you,' said Percy. 'Of course, Diana Punter is a rare exception, but, apart from Diana, I wouldn't give you twopence for the modern girl. She lacks depth and reverence and has no sense of what is fitting. Hats, for example.'

'Exactly. But what do you mean Diana Punter is an exception? She's one of the ringleaders – the spearhead of the movement, if you like to put it that way. Think,' said Nelson, sipping his vermouth, 'of all the unpleasant qualities of the Modern Girl, add them up, double them, and what have you got? Diana Punter. Let me tell you what took place between me and this Punter only a few minutes ago.'

'No,' said Percy. 'Let me tell you what transpired between me and Elizabeth Bottsworth this morning. Nelson, old man, she said my hat – my Bodmin hat – was too small.'

'You don't mean that?'

'Those were her very words.'

'Well, I'm dashed. Listen. Diana Punter told me my equally Bodmin hat was too large.'

They stared at one another.

'It's the Spirit of something,' said Nelson. 'I don't know what, quite, but of something. You see it on all sides. Something very serious has gone wrong with girls nowadays. There is lawlessness and licence abroad.'

'And here in England, too.'

'Well, naturally, you silly ass,' said Nelson, with some asperity. 'When I said abroad, I didn't mean abroad, I meant abroad.'

He mused for a moment.

'I must say, though,' he continued, 'I am surprised at what you tell me about Elizabeth Bottsworth, and am inclined to think there must have been some mistake. I have always been a warm admirer of Elizabeth.'

'And I have always thought Diana one of the best, and I find it hard to believe that she should have shown up in such a dubious light as you suggest. Probably there was a misunderstanding of some kind.'

'Well, I ticked her off properly, anyway.'

Percy Wimbolt shook his head.

'You shouldn't have done that, Nelson. You may have wounded her feelings. In my case, of course, I had no alternative but to be pretty crisp with Elizabeth.'

Nelson Cork clicked his tongue.

'A pity,' he said. 'Elizabeth is sensitive.'

'So is Diana.'

'Not so sensitive as Elizabeth.'

'I should say, at a venture, about five times as sensitive as Elizabeth. However, we must not quarrel about a point like that, old man. The fact that emerges is that we seem both to have been dashed badly treated. I think I shall toddle home and take an aspirin.'

'Me, too.'

They went off to the cloak-room, where their hats were, and Percy put his on.

'Surely,' he said, 'nobody but a half-witted little pip-squeak who can't see straight would say this was too small?'

'It isn't a bit too small,' said Nelson. 'And take a look at this one. Am I not right in supposing that only a female giantess with straws in her hair and astigmatism in both eyes could say it was too large?'

'It's a lovely fit.'

And the cloak-room waiter, a knowledgeable chap of the name of Robinson, said the same.

'So there you are,' said Nelson.

'Ah, well,' said Percy.

They left the club, and parted at the top of Dover Street.

Now, though he had not said so in so many words, Nelson Cork's heart had bled for Percy Wimbolt. He knew the other's fine sensibilities and he could guess how deeply they must have been gashed by this unfortunate breaking-off of diplomatic relations with the girl he loved. For, whatever might have happened, however sorely he might have been wounded, the way Nelson Cork looked at it was that Percy loved Elizabeth Bottsworth in spite of everything. What was required here, felt Nelson, was a tactful mediator – a kindly, sensible friend of both parties who would hitch up his socks and plunge in and heal the breach.

So the moment he had got rid of Percy outside the club he hared round to the house where Elizabeth was staying and was lucky enough to catch her on the front door steps. For, naturally, Elizabeth hadn't gone off to Ascot by herself. Directly Percy was out of sight, she had told the taxi-man to drive her home, and she had been occupying the interval since the painful scene in thinking of things she wished she had said to him and taking her hostess's dog for a run – a Pekingese called Clarkson.

She seemed very pleased to see Nelson, and started to prattle of this and that, her whole demeanour that of a girl who, after having been compelled to associate for a while with the Underworld, has at last found a kindred soul. And the more he listened, the more he wanted to go on listening. And the more he looked at her, the more he felt that a lifetime spent in gazing at Elizabeth Bottsworth would be a lifetime dashed well spent.

There was something about the girl's exquisite petiteness and fragility that appealed to Nelson Cork's depths. After having wasted so much time looking at a female Carnera like Diana Punter, it was a genuine treat to him to be privileged to feast the eyes on one so small and dainty. And, what with one thing and another, he found the most extraordinary difficulty in lugging Percy into the conversation.

They strolled along, chatting. And, mark you, Elizabeth Bottsworth was a girl a fellow could chat with without getting a crick in the neck from goggling up at her, the way you had to do when you took the air with Diana Punter. Nelson realized now that talking to Diana Punter had been like trying to exchange thoughts with a flag-pole sitter. He was surprised that this had never occurred to him before.

'You know, you're looking perfectly ripping, Elizabeth,' he said.

'How funny!' said the girl. 'I was just going to say the same thing about you.'

'Not really?'

'Yes, I was. After some of the gargoyles I've seen today – Percy Wimbolt is an example that springs to the mind – it's such a relief to be with a man who really knows how to turn himself out.'

Now that the Percy *motif* had been introduced, it should have been a simple task for Nelson to turn the talk to the subject of his absent friend. But somehow he didn't. Instead, he just simpered a bit and said: 'Oh no, I say, really, do you mean that?'

'I do, indeed,' said Elizabeth earnestly. 'It's your hat, principally, I think. I don't know why it is, but ever since a child I have been intensely sensitive to hats, and it has always been a pleasure to me to remember that at the age of five I dropped a pot of jam out of the nursery window on to my Uncle Alexander when he came to visit us in a deer-stalker cap with ear-flaps, as worn by Sherlock Holmes. I consider the hat the final test of a man. Now, yours is perfect. I never saw such a beautiful fit. I can't tell you how much I admire that hat. It gives you quite an ambassadorial look.'

Nelson Cork drew a deep breath. He was tingling from head to foot. It was as if the scales had fallen from his eyes and a new life begun for him.

'I say,' he said, trembling with emotion, 'I wonder if you would mind if I pressed your little hand?'

'Do,' said Elizabeth cordially.

22

'I will,' said Nelson, and did so. 'And now,' he went on, clinging to the fin like glue and hiccoughing a bit, 'how about buzzing off somewhere for a quiet cup of tea? I have a feeling that we have much to say to one another.'

It is odd how often it happens in this world that when there are two chaps and one chap's heart is bleeding for the other chap you find that all the while the second chap's heart is bleeding just as much for the first chap. Both bleeding, I mean to say, not only one. It was so in the case of Nelson Cork and Percy Wimbolt. The moment he had left Nelson, Percy charged straight off in search of Diana Punter with the intention of putting everything right with a few well-chosen words.

Because what he felt was that, though at the actual moment of going to press pique might be putting Nelson off Diana, this would pass off and love come into its own again. All that was required, he considered, was a suave go-between, a genial mutual pal who would pour oil on the troubled w.'s and generally fix things up.

He found Diana walking round and round Berkeley Square with her chin up, breathing tensely through the nostrils. He drew up alongside and what-hoed, and as she beheld him the cold, hard gleam in her eyes changed to a light of cordiality. She appeared charmed to see him and at once embarked on an animated conversation. And with every word she spoke his conviction deepened that of all the ways of passing a summer afternoon there was none fruitier than having a friendly hike with Diana Punter.

And it was not only her talk that enchanted him. He was equally fascinated by that wonderful physique of hers. When he considered that he had actually wasted several valuable minutes that day conversing with a young shrimp like Elizabeth Bottsworth, he could have kicked himself.

Here, he reflected, as they walked round the square, was a girl whose ear was more or less on a level with a fellow's mouth, so that such observations as he might make were enabled to get from point to point with the least possible delay. Talking to Elizabeth Bottsworth had always been like bellowing down a well in the hope of attracting the attention of one of the smaller infusoria at the bottom. It surprised him that he had been so long in coming to this conclusion.

He was awakened from this reverie by hearing his companion utter the name of Nelson Cork.

'I beg your pardon?' he said.

'I was saying,' said Diana, 'that Nelson Cork is a wretched little undersized blob who, if he were not too lazy to work, would long since have signed up with some good troupe of midgets.'

'Oh, would you say that?'

'I would say more than that,' said Diana firmly. 'I tell you, Percy, that what makes life so ghastly for girls, what causes girls to get grey hair and go into convents, is the fact that it is not always possible for them to avoid being seen in public with men like Nelson Cork. I trust I am not uncharitable. I try to view these things in a broad-minded way, saying to myself that if a man looks like something that has come out from under a flat stone it is his misfortune rather than his fault and that he is more to be pitied than censured. But on one thing I do insist, that such a man does not wantonly aggravate the natural unpleasantness of his appearance by prancing about London in a hat that reaches down to his ankles. I cannot and will not endure being escorted along Bruton Street by a sort of human bacillus the brim of whose hat bumps on the pavement with every step he takes. What I have always said and what I shall always say is that the hat is the acid test. A man who cannot buy the right-sized hat is a man one could never like or trust. Your hat, now, Percy, is exactly right. I have seen a good many hats in my time, but I really do not think that I have ever come across a more perfect specimen of all that a hat should be. Not too large, not too small, fitting snugly to the head like the skin on a sausage. And you have just the kind of head that a silk hat shows off. It gives you a sort of look . . . how shall I describe it? . . . it conveys the idea of a master of men. Leonine is the word I want. There is something about the way it rests on the brow and the almost imperceptible tilt towards the south-east . . .'

Percy Wimbolt was quivering like an Oriental muscle-dancer. Soft music seemed to be playing from the direction of Hay Hill, and Berkeley Square had begun to skip round him on one foot.

He drew a deep breath.

'I say,' he said, 'stop me if you've heard this before, but what I feel we ought to do at this juncture is to dash off somewhere where it's quiet and there aren't so many houses dancing the "Blue Danube" and shove some tea into ourselves. And over the pot and muffins I shall have something very important to say to you.'

'So that,' concluded the Crumpet, taking a grape, 'is how the thing stands; and, in a sense, of course, you could say that it is a satisfactory ending.

'The announcement of Elizabeth's engagement to Nelson Cork appeared in the Press on the same day as that of Diana's projected hitching-up with Percy Wimbolt: and it is pleasant that the happy couples should be so well matched as regards size.

'I mean to say, there will be none of that business of a six-foot girl tripping down the aisle with a five-foot-four man, or a six-foot-two man trying to keep step along the sacred edifice with a four-foot-three girl. This is always good for a laugh from the ringside pews, but it does not make for wedded bliss.

'No, as far as the principals are concerned, we may say that all has ended well. But that doesn't seem to me the important point. What seems to me the important point is this extraordinary, baffling mystery of those hats.'

'Absolutely,' said the Bean.

'I mean to say, if Percy's hat really didn't fit, as

Elizabeth Bottsworth contended, why should it have registered as a winner with Diana Punter?'

'Absolutely,' said the Bean.

'And, conversely, if Nelson's hat was the total loss which Diana Punter considered it, why, only a brief while later, was it going like a breeze with Elizabeth Bottsworth?'

'Absolutely,' said the Bean.

'The whole thing is utterly inscrutable.'

It was at this point that the nurse gave signs of wishing to catch the Speaker's eye.

'Shall I tell you what I think?'

'Say on, my dear young pillow-smoother.'

'I believe Bodmin's boy must have got those hats mixed. When he was putting them back in the boxes, I mean.'

The Crumpet shook his head, and took a grape.

'And then at the club they got the right ones again.'

The Crumpet smiled indulgently.

'Ingenious,' he said, taking a grape. 'Quite ingenious. But a little far-fetched. No, I prefer to think the whole thing, as I say, has something to do with the Fourth Dimension. I am convinced that that is the true explanation, if our minds could only grasp it.'

'Absolutely,' said the Bean.

UNCLE FRED FLITS BY

In order that they might enjoy their afternoon luncheon coffee in peace, the Crumpet had taken the guest whom he was entertaining at the Drones Club to the smaller and less frequented of the two smoking-rooms. In the other, he explained, though the conversation always touched an exceptionally high level of brilliance, there was apt to be a good deal of sugar thrown about.

The guest said he understood.

'Young blood, eh?'

'That's right. Young blood.'

'And animal spirits.'

'And animal, as you say, spirits,' agreed the Crumpet. 'We get a fairish amount of those here.'

'The complaint, however, is not, I observe, universal.'

'Eh?'

The other drew his host's attention to the doorway, where a young man in form-fitting tweeds had just appeared. The aspect of this young man was haggard. His eyes glared wildly and he sucked at an empty cigarette-holder. If he had a mind, there was something on it. When the Crumpet called to him to come and join the party, he merely shook his head in a distraught sort of way and disappeared, looking like a character out of a Greek tragedy pursued by the Fates.

The Crumpet sighed. 'Poor old Pongo!'

'Pongo?'

'That was Pongo Twistleton. He's all broken up about his Uncle Fred.'

'Dead?'

'No such luck. Coming up to London again tomorrow. Pongo had a wire this morning.'

'And that upsets him?'

'Naturally. After what happened last time.'

'What was that?'

'Ah!' said the Crumpet.

'What happened last time?'

'You may well ask.'

'I do ask.'

'Ah!' said the Crumpet.

Poor old Pongo (said the Crumpet) has often discussed his Uncle Fred with me, and if there weren't tears in his eyes when he did so, I don't know a tear in the eye when I see one. In round numbers the Earl of Ickenham, of Ickenham Hall, Ickenham, Hants, he lives in the country most of the year, but from time to time has a nasty way of slipping his collar and getting loose and descending upon Pongo at his flat in the Albany. And every time he does so, the unhappy young blighter is subjected to some soul-testing experience. Because the trouble with this uncle is that, though sixty if a day, he becomes on arriving in the metropolis as young as he feels – which is, apparently, a youngish twenty-two. I don't know if you happen to know what the word 'excesses' means, but those are what Pongo's Uncle Fred from the country, when in London, invariably commits.

It wouldn't so much matter, mind you, if he would confine his activities to the club premises. We're pretty broad-minded here, and if you stop short of smashing the piano, there isn't much that you can do at the Drones that will cause the raised eyebrow and the sharp intake of breath. The snag is that he will insist on lugging Pongo out in the open and there, right in the public eye, proceeding to step high, wide and plentiful.

So when, on the occasion to which I allude, he stood pink and genial on Pongo's hearth-rug, bulging with Pongo's lunch and wreathed in the smoke of one of Pongo's cigars, and said: 'And now, my boy, for a pleasant and instructive afternoon,' you will readily understand why the unfortunate young clam gazed at him as he would have gazed at two-penn'orth of dynamite, had he discovered it lighting up in his presence.

'A what?' he said, giving at the knees and paling beneath the tan a bit.

'A pleasant and instructive afternoon,' repeated Lord Ickenham, rolling the words round his tongue. 'I propose that you place yourself in my hands and leave the programme entirely to me.'

Now, owing to Pongo's circumstances being such as to necessitate his getting into the aged relative's ribs at intervals and shaking him down for an occasional much-needed tenner or what not, he isn't in a position to use the iron hand with the old buster. But at these words he displayed a manly firmness.

'You aren't going to get me to the dog races again.'

'No, no.'

'You remember what happened last June.'

'Quite,' said Lord Ickenham, 'quite. Though I still think that a wiser magistrate would have been content with a mere reprimand.'

'And I won't—'

'Certainly not. Nothing of that kind at all. What I propose to do this afternoon is to take you to visit the home of your ancestors.'

Pongo did not get this.

'I thought Ickenham was the home of my ancestors.'

'It is one of the homes of your ancestors. They also resided rather nearer the heart of things, at a place called Mitching Hill.'

'Down in the suburbs, do you mean?'

'The neighbourhood is now suburban, true. It is many years since the meadows where I sported as a child were sold and cut up into building lots. But when I was a boy Mitching Hill was open country. It was a vast, rolling estate belonging to your great-uncle, Marmaduke, a man with whiskers of a nature which you with your pure mind would scarcely credit, and I have long felt a sentimental urge to see what the hell the old place looks like now. Perfectly foul, I expect. Still, I think we should make the pious pilgrimage.'

Pongo absolutely-ed heartily. He was all for the scheme. A great weight seemed to have rolled off his mind. The way he looked at it was that even an uncle within a short jump of the loony bin couldn't very well get into much trouble in a suburb. I mean, you know what suburbs are. They don't, as it were, offer the scope. One follows his reasoning, of course.

'Fine!' he said. 'Splendid! Topping!'

'Then put on your hat and rompers, my boy,' said Lord Ickenham, 'and let us be off. I fancy one gets there by omnibuses and things.'

Well, Pongo hadn't expected much in the way of mental uplift from the sight of Mitching Hill, and he didn't get it. Alighting from the bus, he tells me, you found yourself in the middle of rows and rows of semi-detached villas, all looking exactly alike, and you went on and you came to more semi-detached villas, and those all looked exactly alike, too. Nevertheless, he did not repine. It was one of those early spring days which suddenly change to mid-winter and he had come out without his overcoat, and it looked like rain and he hadn't an umbrella, but despite this his mood was one of sober ecstasy. The hours were passing and his uncle had not yet made a goat of himself. At the Dog Races the other had been in the hands of the constabulary in the first ten minutes.

It began to seem to Pongo that with any luck he might be able to keep the old blister pottering harmlessly about here till nightfall, when he could shoot a bit of dinner into him and put him to bed. And as Lord Ickenham had specifically stated that his wife, Pongo's Aunt Jane, had expressed her intention of scalping him with a blunt knife if he wasn't back at the Hall by lunchtime on the morrow, it really looked as if he might get through this visit without perpetrating a single major outrage on the public weal. It is rather interesting to note that as he thought this Pongo smiled, because it was the last time he smiled that day.

All this while, I should mention, Lord Ickenham had been stopping at intervals like a pointing dog and saying that it must have been just about here that he plugged the gardener in the trousers seat with his bow and arrow and that over there he had been sick after his first cigar, and he now paused in front of a villa which for some unknown reason called itself The Cedars. His face was tender and wistful.

'On this very spot, if I am not mistaken,' he said, heaving a bit of a sigh, 'on this very spot, fifty years ago come Lammas Eve, I . . . Oh, blast it!'

The concluding remark had been caused by the fact that the rain, which had held off until now, suddenly began to buzz down like a shower-bath. With no further words, they leaped into the porch of the villa and there took shelter, exchanging glances with a grey parrot which hung in a cage in the window.

Not that you could really call it shelter. They were protected from above all right, but the moisture was now falling with a sort of swivel action, whipping in through the sides of the porch and tickling them up properly. And it was just after Pongo had turned up his collar and was huddling against the door that the door gave way. From the fact that a female of general-servant aspect was standing there he gathered that his uncle must have rung the bell.

This female wore a long mackintosh, and Lord Ickenham beamed upon her with a fairish spot of suavity.

'Good afternoon,' he said.

The female said good afternoon.

'The Cedars?'

The female said yes, it was The Cedars.

'Are the old folks at home?'

The female said there was nobody at home.

'Ah? Well, never mind. I have come,' said Lord Ickenham, edging in, 'to clip the parrot's claws. My assistant, Mr Walkinshaw, who applies the anaesthetic,' he added, indicating Pongo with a gesture.

'Are you from the bird shop?'

'A very happy guess.'

'Nobody told me you were coming.'

'They keep things from you, do they?' said Lord Ickenham, sympathetically. 'Too bad.'

Continuing to edge, he had got into the parlour by now, Pongo following in a sort of dream and the female following Pongo.

'Well, I suppose it's all right,' she said. 'I was just going out. It's my afternoon.'

'Go out,' said Lord Ickenham cordially. 'By all means go out. We will leave everything in order.'

And presently the female, though still a bit on the dubious side, pushed off, and Lord Ickenham lit the gas-fire and drew a chair up.

'So here we are, my boy,' he said. 'A little tact, a little address, and here we are, snug and cosy and not catching our deaths of cold. You'll never go far wrong if you leave things to me.'

'But, dash it, we can't stop here,' said Pongo.

Lord Ickenham raised his eyebrows.

'Not stop here? Are you suggesting that we go out into that rain? My dear lad, you are not aware of the grave issues involved. This morning, as I was leaving home, I had a rather painful disagreement with your aunt. She said the weather was treacherous and wished me to take my woolly muffler. I replied that the weather was not treacherous and that I would be dashed if I took my woolly muffler. Eventually, by the exercise of an iron will, I had my way, and I ask you, my dear boy, to envisage what will happen if I return with a cold in the head. I shall sink to the level of a fifth-class power. Next time I came to London, it would be with a liver pad and a respirator. No! I shall remain here, toasting my toes at this really excellent fire. I had no idea that a gas-fire radiated such warmth. I feel all in a glow.'

So did Pongo. His brow was wet with honest sweat. He is reading for the Bar, and while he would be the first to admit that he hasn't yet got a complete toe-hold on the Law of Great Britain he had a sort of notion that oiling into a perfect stranger's semi-detached villa on the pretext of pruning the parrot was a tort or misdemeanour, if not actual barratry or soccage in fief or something like that. And apart from the legal aspect of the matter there was the embarrassment of the thing. Nobody is more of a whale on correctness and not doing what's not done than Pongo, and the situation in which he now found himself caused him to chew the lower lip and, as I say, perspire a goodish deal.

'But suppose the blighter who owns this ghastly house comes back?' he asked. 'Talking of envisaging things, try that one over on your pianola.'

And, sure enough, as he spoke, the front door bell rang.

'There!' said Pongo.

'Don't say "There!" my boy,' said Lord Ickenham reprovingly. 'It's the sort of thing your aunt says. I see no reason for alarm. Obviously this is some casual caller. A ratepayer would have used his latchkey. Glance cautiously out of the window and see if you can see anybody.'

'It's a pink chap,' said Pongo, having done so.

'How pink?'

'Pretty pink.'

'Well, there you are, then. I told you so. It can't be the big chief. The sort of fellows who own houses like this are pale and sallow, owing to working in offices all day. Go and see what he wants.'

'You go and see what he wants.'

'We'll both go and see what he wants,' said Lord Ickenham.

So they went and opened the front door, and there, as Pongo had said, was a pink chap. A small young pink chap, a bit moist about the shoulder-blades.

'Pardon me,' said this pink chap, 'is Mr Roddis in?'

'No,' said Pongo.

'Yes,' said Lord Ickenham. 'Don't be silly, Douglas – of course I'm in. I am Mr Roddis,' he said to the pink chap. 'This, such as he is, is my son Douglas. And you?'

'Name of Robinson.'

'What about it?'

'My name's Robinson.'

'Oh, *your* name's Robinson? Now we've got it straight. Delighted to see you, Mr Robinson. Come right in and take your boots off.'

They all trickled back to the parlour, Lord Ickenham pointing out objects of interest by the wayside to the chap, Pongo gulping for air a bit and trying to get himself abreast of this new twist in the scenario. His heart was becoming more and more bowed down with weight of woe. He hadn't liked being Mr Walkinshaw, the anaesthetist, and he didn't like it any better being

Roddis Junior. In brief, he feared the worst. It was only too plain to him by now that his uncle had got it thoroughly up his nose and had settled down to one of his big afternoons, and he was asking himself, as he had so often asked himself before, what would the harvest be?

Arrived in the parlour, the pink chap proceeded to stand on one leg and look coy.

'Is Julia here?' he asked, simpering a bit, Pongo says.

'Is she?' said Lord Ickenham to Pongo.

'No,' said Pongo.

'No,' said Lord Ickenham.

'She wired me she was coming here today.'

'Ah, then we shall have a bridge four.'

The pink chap stood on the other leg.

'I don't suppose you've ever met Julia. Bit of trouble in the family, she gave me to understand.'

'It is often the way.'

'The Julia I mean is your niece Julia Parker. Or, rather, your wife's niece Julia Parker.'

'Any niece of my wife is a niece of mine,' said Lord Ickenham heartily. 'We share and share alike.'

'Julia and I want to get married.'

'Well, go ahead.'

'But they won't let us.'

'Who won't?'

'Her mother and father. And Uncle Charlie Parker and Uncle Henry Parker and the rest of them. They don't think I'm good enough.'

'The morality of the modern young man is notoriously lax.'

'Class enough, I mean. They're a haughty lot.'

'What makes them haughty? Are they earls?'

'No, they aren't earls.'

'Then why the devil,' said Lord Ickenham warmly, 'are they haughty? Only earls have a right to be haughty. Earls are hot stuff. When you get an earl, you've got something.'

'Besides, we've had words. Me and her father. One thing led to another, and in the end I called him a perishing old— Coo!' said the pink chap, breaking off suddenly.

He had been standing by the window, and he now leaped lissomely into the middle of the room, causing Pongo, whose nervous system was by this time definitely down among the wines and spirits and who hadn't been expecting this *adagio* stuff, to bite his tongue with some severity.

'They're on the doorstep! Julia and her mother and father. I didn't know they were all coming.'

'You do not wish to meet them?'

'No, I don't!'

'Then duck behind the settee, Mr Robinson,' said Lord Ickenham, and the pink chap, weighing the advice and finding it good, did so. And as he disappeared the door bell rang.

Once more, Lord Ickenham led Pongo out into the hall.

'I say!' said Pongo, and a close observer might have noted that he was quivering like an aspen.

'Say on, my dear boy.'

'I mean to say, what?'

'What?'

'You aren't going to let these bounders in, are you?'

'Certainly,' said Lord Ickenham. 'We Roddises keep open house. And as they are presumably aware that Mr Roddis has no son, I think we had better return to the old layout. You are the local vet, my boy, come to minister to my parrot. When I return, I should like to find you by the cage, staring at the bird in a scientific manner. Tap your teeth from time to time with a pencil and try to smell of iodoform. It will help to add conviction.'

So Pongo shifted back to the parrot's cage and stared so earnestly that it was only when a voice said 'Well!' that he became aware that there was anybody in the room. Turning, he perceived that Hampshire's leading curse had come back, bringing the gang.

It consisted of a stern, thin, middle-aged woman, a middle-aged man and a girl.

You can generally accept Pongo's estimate of girls, and when he says that this one was a pippin one knows that he uses the term in its most exact sense. She was about nineteen, he thinks, and she wore a black beret, a dark-green leather coat, a shortish tweed skirt, silk stockings and high-heeled shoes. Her eyes were large and lustrous and her face like a dewy rosebud at daybreak on a June morning. So Pongo tells me. Not that I suppose he has ever seen a rosebud at daybreak on a June morning, because it's generally as much as you can do to lug him out of bed in time for nine-thirty breakfast. Still, one gets the idea.

'Well,' said the woman, 'you don't know who I am, I'll be bound. I'm Laura's sister Connie. This is Claude, my husband. And this is my daughter Julia. Is Laura in?'

'I regret to say, no,' said Lord Ickenham.

The woman was looking at him as if he didn't come up to her specifications.

'I thought you were younger,' she said.

'Younger than what?' said Lord Ickenham.

'Younger than you are.'

'You can't be younger than you are, worse luck,' said Lord Ickenham. 'Still, one does one's best, and I am bound to say that of recent years I have made a pretty good go of it.'

The woman caught sight of Pongo, and he didn't seem to please her, either.

'Who's that?'

'The local vet, clustering round my parrot.'

'I can't talk in front of him.'

'It is quite all right,' Lord Ickenham assured her. 'The poor fellow is stone deaf.'

And with an imperious gesture at Pongo, as much as to bid him stare less at girls and more at parrots, he got the company seated.

'Now, then,' he said.

There was silence for a moment, then a sort of

muffled sob, which Pongo thinks proceeded from the girl. He couldn't see, of course, because his back was turned and he was looking at the parrot, which looked back at him — most offensively, he says, as parrots will, using one eye only for the purpose. It also asked him to have a nut.

The woman came into action again.

'Although,' she said, 'Laura never did me the honour to invite me to her wedding, for which reason I have not communicated with her for five years, necessity compels me to cross her threshold today. There comes a time when differences must be forgotten and relatives must stand shoulder to shoulder.'

'I see what you mean,' said Lord Ickenham. 'Like the boys of the old brigade.'

'What I say is, let bygones be bygones. I would not have intruded on you, but needs must. I disregard the past and appeal to your sense of pity.'

The thing began to look to Pongo like a touch, and he is convinced that the parrot thought so, too, for it winked and cleared its throat. But they were both wrong. The woman went on.

'I want you and Laura to take Julia into your home for a week or so, until I can make other arrangements for her. Julia is studying the piano, and she sits for her examination in two weeks' time, so until then she must remain in London. The trouble is, she has fallen in love. Or thinks she has.'

'I know I have,' said Julia.

Her voice was so attractive that Pongo was compelled to slew round and take another look at her. Her eyes, he says, were shining like twin stars and there was a sort of Soul's Awakening expression on her face, and what the dickens there was in a pink chap like the pink chap, who even as pink chaps go wasn't much of a pink chap, to make her look like that, was frankly, Pongo says, more than he could understand. The thing baffled him. He sought in vain for a solution.

'Yesterday, Claude and I arrived in London from our Bexhill home to give Julia a pleasant surprise. We stayed, naturally, in the boarding-house where she has been living for the past six weeks. And what do you think we discovered?'

'Insects.'

'Not insects. A letter. From a young man. I found to my horror that a young man of whom I knew nothing was arranging to marry my daughter. I sent for him immediately, and found him to be quite impossible. He jellies eels!'

'Does what?'

'He is an assistant at a jellied eel shop.'

'But surely,' said Lord Ickenham, 'that speaks well for him. The capacity to jelly an eel seems to me to argue intelligence of a high order. It isn't everybody who can do it, by any means. I know if someone came to me and said, "Jelly this eel!" I should be nonplussed. And so, or I am very much mistaken, would Ramsay MacDonald and Winston Churchill.'

The woman did not seem to see eye to eye.

'Tchah!' she said. 'What do you suppose my husband's brother Charlie Parker would say if I allowed his niece to marry a man who jellies eels?'

'Ah!' said Claude, who, before we go any further, was a tall, drooping bird with a red soup-strainer moustache.

'Or my husband's brother, Henry Parker.'

'Ah!' said Claude. 'Or Cousin Alf Robbins, for that matter.'

'Exactly. Cousin Alfred would die of shame.'

The girl Julia hiccoughed passionately, so much so that Pongo says it was all he could do to stop himself nipping across and taking her hand in his and patting it.

'I've told you a hundred times, Mother, that Wilberforce is only jellying eels till he finds something better.'

'What is better than an eel?' asked Lord Ickenham, who had been following this discussion with the close attention it deserved. 'For jellying purposes, I mean.'

'He is ambitious. It won't be long,' said the girl, 'before Wilberforce suddenly rises in the world.'

She never spoke a truer word. At this very moment, up he came from behind the settee like a leaping salmon.

'Julia!' he cried.

'Wilby!' yipped the girl.

And Pongo says he never saw anything more sickening in his life than the way she flung herself into the blighter's arms and clung there like the ivy on the old garden wall. It wasn't that he had anything specific against the pink chap, but this girl had made a deep impression on him and he resented her glueing herself to another in this manner.

Julia's mother, after just that brief moment which a woman needs in which to recover from her natural surprise at seeing eel-jelliers pop up from behind sofas, got moving and plucked her away like a referee breaking a couple of welter-weights.

'Julia Parker,' she said, 'I'm ashamed of you!'

'So am I,' said Claude.

'I blush for you.'

'Me, too,' said Claude. 'Hugging and kissing a man who called your father a perishing old bottle-nosed Gawd-help-us.'

'I think,' said Lord Ickenham, shoving his oar in, 'that before proceeding any further we ought to go into that point. If he called you a perishing old bottle-nosed Gawd-help-us, it seems to me that the first thing to do is to decide whether he was right, and frankly, in my opinion . . .'

'Wilberforce will apologize.'

'Certainly I'll apologize. It isn't fair to hold a remark passed in the heat of the moment against a chap . . .'

'Mr Robinson,' said the woman, 'you know perfectly well that whatever remarks you may have seen fit to pass don't matter one way or the other. If you were listening to what I was saying you will understand . . .'

'Oh, I know, I know. Uncle Charlie Parker and

Uncle Henry Parker and Cousin Alf Robbins and all that. Pack of snobs!'

'What!'

'Haughty, stuck-up snobs. Them and their class distinction. Think themselves everybody just because they've got money. I'd like to know how they got it.'

'What do you mean by that?'

'Never mind what I mean.'

'If you are insinuating—'

'Well, of course, you know, Connie,' said Lord Ickenham mildly, 'he's quite right. You can't get away from that.'

I don't know if you have ever seen a bull-terrier embarking on a scrap with an Airedale and just as it was getting down nicely to its work suddenly having an unexpected Kerry Blue sneak up behind it and bite it in the rear quarters. When this happens, it lets go of the Airedale and swivels round and fixes the butting-in animal with a pretty nasty eye. It was exactly the same with the woman Connie when Lord Ickenham spoke these words.

'What!'

'I was only wondering if you had forgotten how Charlie Parker made his pile.'

'What are you talking about?'

'I know it is painful,' said Lord Ickenham, 'and one doesn't mention it as a rule, but, as we are on the subject, you must admit that lending money at two hundred and fifty per cent interest is not done in the best circles. The judge, if you remember, said so at the trial.'

'I never knew that!' cried the girl Julia.

'Ah,' said Lord Ickenham. 'You kept it from the child? Quite right, quite right.'

'It's a lie!'

'And when Henry Parker had all that fuss with the bank it was touch and go they didn't send him to prison. Between ourselves, Connie, has a bank official, even a brother of your husband, any right to sneak fifty pounds from the till in order to put it on a hundred to one shot for the Grand National? Not quite playing the game, Connie. Not the straight bat. Henry, I grant you, won five thousand of the best and never looked back afterwards, but, though we applaud his judgment of form, we must surely look askance at his financial methods. As for Cousin Alf Robbins . . .'

The woman was making rummy stuttering sounds. Pongo tells me he once had a Pommery Seven which used to express itself in much the same way if you tried to get it to take a hill on high. A sort of mixture of gurgles and explosions.

'There is not a word of truth in this,' she gasped at length, having managed to get the vocal cords disentangled. 'Not a single word. I think you must have gone mad.'

Lord Ickenham shrugged his shoulders.

'Have it your own way, Connie. I was only going to say that, while the jury were probably compelled on

the evidence submitted to them to give Cousin Alf
Robbins the benefit of the doubt when charged with
smuggling dope, everybody knew that he had been
doing it for years. I am not blaming him, mind you. If
a man can smuggle cocaine and get away with it, good
luck to him, say I. The only point I am trying to make
is that we are hardly a family that can afford to put on
dog and sneer at honest suitors for our daughters'
hands. Speaking for myself, I consider that we are very
lucky to have the chance of marrying even into eel-
jellying circles.'

'So do I,' said Julia firmly.

'You don't believe what this man is saying?'

'I believe every word.'

'So do I,' said the pink chap.

The woman snorted. She seemed overwrought.

'Well,' she said, 'goodness knows I have never liked
Laura, but I would never have wished her a husband
like you!'

'Husband?' said Lord Ickenham, puzzled. 'What
gives you the impression that Laura and I are married?'

There was a weighty silence, during which the parrot threw out a general invitation to join it in a nut.
Then the girl Julia spoke.

'You'll have to let me marry Wilberforce now,' she
said. 'He knows too much about us.'

'I was rather thinking that myself,' said Lord Ickenham. 'Seal his lips, I say.'

'You wouldn't mind marrying into a low family,

would you, darling?' asked the girl, with a touch of anxiety.

'No family could be too low for me, dearest, if it was yours,' said the pink chap.

'After all, we needn't see them.'

'That's right.'

'It isn't one's relations that matter: it's oneselves.'

'That's right, too.'

'Wilby!'

'Julia!'

They repeated the old ivy on the garden wall act. Pongo says he didn't like it any better than the first time, but his distaste wasn't in it with the woman Connie's.

'And what, may I ask,' she said, 'do you propose to marry on?'

This seemed to cast a damper. They came apart. They looked at each other. The girl looked at the pink chap, and the pink chap looked at the girl. You could see that a jarring note had been struck.

'Wilberforce is going to be a very rich man some day.'

'Some day!'

'If I had a hundred pounds,' said the pink chap, 'I could buy a half-share in one of the best milk walks in South London tomorrow.'

'If!' said the woman.

'Ah!' said Claude.

'Where are you going to get it?'

'Ah!' said Claude.

'Where,' repeated the woman, plainly pleased with the snappy crack and loath to let it ride without an encore, 'are you going to get it?'

'That,' said Claude, 'is the point. Where are you going to get a hundred pounds?'

'Why, bless my soul,' said Lord Ickenham jovially, 'from me, of course. Where else?'

And before Pongo's bulging eyes he fished out from the recesses of his costume a crackling bundle of notes and handed it over. And the agony of realizing that the old bounder had had all that stuff on him all this time and that he hadn't touched him for so much as a tithe of it was so keen, Pongo says, that before he knew what he was doing he had let out a sharp, whinnying cry which rang through the room like the yowl of a stepped-on puppy.

'Ah,' said Lord Ickenham. 'The vet wishes to speak to me. Yes, vet?'

This seemed to puzzle the cerise bloke a bit.

'I thought you said this chap was your son.'

'If I had a son,' said Lord Ickenham, a little hurt, 'he would be a good deal better-looking than that. No, this is the local veterinary surgeon. I may have said I *looked* on him as a son. Perhaps that was what confused you.'

He shifted across to Pongo and twiddled his hands enquiringly. Pongo gaped at him, and it was not until one of the hands caught him smartly in the lower ribs that he remembered he was deaf and started to twiddle back. Considering that he wasn't supposed to be dumb,

I can't see why he should have twiddled, but no doubt there are moments when twiddling is about all a fellow feels himself equal to. For what seemed to him at least ten hours Pongo had been undergoing great mental stress, and one can't blame him for not being chatty. Anyway, be that as it may, he twiddled.

'I cannot quite understand what he says,' announced Lord Ickenham at length, 'because he sprained a finger this morning and that makes him stammer. But I gather that he wishes to have a word with me in private. Possibly my parrot has got something the matter with it which he is reluctant to mention even in sign language in front of a young unmarried girl. You know what parrots are. We will step outside.'

'*We* will step outside,' said Wilberforce.

'Yes,' said the girl Julia. 'I feel like a walk.'

'And you,' said Lord Ickenham to the woman Connie, who was looking like a female Napoleon at Moscow. 'Do you join the hikers?'

'I shall remain and make myself a cup of tea. You will not grudge us a cup of tea, I hope?'

'Far from it,' said Lord Ickenham cordially. 'This is Liberty Hall. Stick around and mop it up till your eyes bubble.'

Outside, the girl, looking more like a dewy rosebud than ever, fawned on the old buster pretty considerably.

'I don't know how to thank you!' she said. And the pink chap said he didn't, either.

'Not at all, my dear, not at all,' said Lord Ickenham.

'I think you're simply wonderful.'

'No, no.'

'You are. Perfectly marvellous.'

'Tut, tut,' said Lord Ickenham. 'Don't give the matter another thought.'

He kissed her on both cheeks, the chin, the forehead, the right eyebrow, and the tip of the nose, Pongo looking on the while in a baffled and discontented manner. Everybody seemed to be kissing this girl except him.

Eventually the degrading spectacle ceased and the girl and the pink chap shoved off, and Pongo was enabled to take up the matter of that hundred quid.

'Where,' he asked, 'did you get all that money?'

'Now, where did I?' mused Lord Ickenham. 'I know your aunt gave it to me for some purpose. But what? To pay some bill or other, I rather fancy.'

This cheered Pongo up slightly.

'She'll give you the devil when you get back,' he said, with not a little relish. 'I wouldn't be in your shoes for something. When you tell Aunt Jane,' he said, with confidence, for he knew his Aunt Jane's emotional nature, 'that you slipped her entire roll to a girl, and explain, as you will have to explain, that she was an extraordinarily pretty girl – a girl, in fine, who looked like something out of a beauty chorus of the better sort, I should think she would pluck down one of the ancestral battle-axes from the wall and jolly well strike you on the mazzard.'

'Have no anxiety, my dear boy,' said Lord Ickenham.

'It is like your kind heart to be so concerned, but have no anxiety. I shall tell her that I was compelled to give the money to you to enable you to buy back some compromising letters from a Spanish *demi-mondaine*. She will scarcely be able to blame me for rescuing a fondly-loved nephew from the clutches of an adventuress. It may be that she will feel a little vexed with you for a while, and that you may have to allow a certain time to elapse before you visit Ickenham again, but then I shan't be wanting you at Ickenham till the ratting season starts, so all is well.'

At this moment, there came toddling up to the gate of The Cedars a large red-faced man. He was just going in when Lord Ickenham hailed him.

'Mr Roddis?'

'Hey?'

'Am I addressing Mr Roddis?'

'That's me.'

'I am Mr J. G. Bulstrode from down the road,' said Lord Ickenham. 'This is my sister's husband's brother, Percy Frensham, in the lard and imported-butter business.'

The red-faced bird said he was pleased to meet them. He asked Pongo if things were brisk in the lard and imported-butter business, and Pongo said they were all right, and the red-faced bird said he was glad to hear it.

'We have never met, Mr Roddis,' said Lord Ickenham, 'but I think it would be only neighbourly to inform you that a short while ago I observed two suspicious-looking persons in your house.'

'In my house? How on earth did they get there?'

'No doubt through a window at the back. They looked to me like cat burglars. If you creep up, you may be able to see them.'

The red-faced bird crept, and came back not exactly foaming at the mouth but with the air of a man who for two pins would so foam.

'You're perfectly right. They're sitting in my parlour as cool as dammit, swigging my tea and buttered toast.'

'I thought as much.'

'And they've opened a pot of my raspberry jam.'

'Ah, then you will be able to catch them red-handed. I should fetch a policeman.'

'I will. Thank you, Mr Bulstrode.'

'Only too glad to have been able to render you this little service, Mr Roddis,' said Lord Ickenham. 'Well, I must be moving. I have an appointment. Pleasant after the rain, is it not? Come, Percy.'

He lugged Pongo off.

'So that,' he said, with satisfaction, 'is that. On these visits of mine to the metropolis, my boy, I always make it my aim, if possible, to spread sweetness and light. I look about me, even in a foul hole like Mitching Hill, and I ask myself – How can I leave this foul hole a better and happier foul hole than I found it? And if I see a chance, I grab it. Here is our omnibus. Spring aboard, my boy, and on our way home we will be sketching out rough plans for the evening. If the old Leicester Grill is still in existence, we might look in there. It must be fully thirty-five years since I was last thrown out of the Leicester Grill. I wonder who is the bouncer there now.'

Such (concluded the Crumpet) is Pongo Twistleton's Uncle Fred from the country, and you will have gathered by now a rough notion of why it is that when a telegram comes announcing his impending arrival in the great city Pongo blenches to the core and calls for a couple of quick ones.

The whole situation, Pongo says, is very complex. Looking at it from one angle, it is fine that the man lives in the country most of the year. If he didn't, he would have him in his midst all the time. On the other hand, by living in the country he generates, as it were, a store of loopiness which expends itself with frightful violence on his rare visits to the centre of things.

What it boils down to is this – Is it better to have a loopy uncle whose loopiness is perpetually on tap but spread out thin, so to speak, or one who lies low in distant Hants for three hundred and sixty days in the year and does himself proud in London for the other five? Dashed moot, of course, and Pongo has never been able to make up his mind on the point.

Naturally, the ideal thing would be if someone would chain the old hound up permanently and keep

him from Jan. One to Dec. Thirty-one where he
wouldn't do any harm — viz. among the spuds and ten-
antry. But this, Pongo admits, is a Utopian dream.
Nobody could work harder to that end than his Aunt
Jane, and she has never been able to manage it.

TROUBLE DOWN AT TUDSLEIGH

Two Eggs and a couple of Beans were having a leisurely spot in the smoking-room of the Drones Club, when a Crumpet came in and asked if anybody present wished to buy a practically new copy of Tennyson's poems. His manner, as he spoke, suggested that he had little hope that business would result. Nor did it. The two Beans and one of the Eggs said No. The other Egg merely gave a short, sardonic laugh.

The Crumpet hastened to put himself right with the Company.

'It isn't mine. It belongs to Freddie Widgeon.'

The senior of the two Beans drew his breath in sharply, genuinely shocked.

'You aren't telling us Freddie Widgeon bought a Tennyson?'

The junior Bean said that this confirmed a suspicion which had long been stealing over him. Poor old Freddie was breaking up.

'Not at all,' said the Crumpet. 'He had the most

excellent motives. The whole thing was a strategic move, and in my opinion a jolly fine strategic move. He did it to boost his stock with the girl.'

'What girl?'

'April Carroway. She lived at a place called Tudsleigh down in Worcestershire. Freddie went there for the fishing, and the day he left London he happened to run into his uncle, Lord Blicester, and the latter, learning that he was to be in those parts, told him on no account to omit to look in at Tudsleigh Court and slap his old friend, Lady Carroway, on the back. So Freddie called there on the afternoon of his arrival, to get the thing over: and as he was passing through the garden on his way out he suddenly heard a girl's voice proceeding from the interior of a summer-house. And so musical was it that he edged a bit closer and shot a glance through the window. And, as he did so, he reeled and came within a toucher of falling.'

From where he stood he could see the girl plainly, and she was, he tells me, the absolute ultimate word, the last bubbling cry. She could not have looked better to him if he had drawn up the specifications personally. He was stunned. He had had no idea that there was anything like this on the premises. There and then he abandoned his scheme of spending the next two weeks fishing: for day by day in every way, he realized, he must haunt Tudsleigh Court from now on like a resident spectre.

He had now recovered sufficiently for his senses to function once more, and he gathered that what the girl was doing was reading some species of poetry aloud to a small, grave female kid with green eyes and turned-up nose who sat at her side. And the idea came to him that it would be a pretty sound scheme if he could find out what this bilge was. For, of course, when it comes to wooing, it's simply half the battle to get a line on the adored object's favourite literature. Ascertain what it is and mug it up and decant an excerpt or two in her presence, and before you can say 'What ho!' she is looking on you as a kindred soul and is all over you.

And it was at this point that he had a nice little slice of luck. The girl suddenly stopped reading: and, placing the volume face-down on her lap, sat gazing dreamily nor'-nor'-east for a space, as I believe girls frequently do when they strike a particularly juicy bit half-way through a poem. And the next moment Freddie was hareing off to the local post-office to wire to London for a *Collected Works of Alfred, Lord Tennyson*. He was rather relieved, he tells me, because, girls being what they are, it might quite easily have been Shelley or even Browning.

Well, Freddie lost no time in putting into operation his scheme of becoming the leading pest at Tudsleigh Court. On the following afternoon he called there again, met Lady Carroway once more, and was introduced to this girl, April, and to the green-eyed kid, who, he learned, was her young sister Prudence. So far, so good. But just as he was starting to direct at April a respectfully volcanic look which would give her some rough kind of preliminary intimation that here came old Colonel Romeo in person, his hostess went on to say something which sounded like 'Captain Bradbury,' and he perceived with a nasty shock that he was not the only visitor. Seated in a chair with a cup of tea in one hand and half a muffin in the other was an extraordinarily large and beefy bird in tweeds.

'Captain Bradbury, Mr Widgeon,' said Lady Carroway. 'Captain Bradbury is in the Indian Army. He is home on leave and has taken a house up the river.'

'Oh?' said Freddie, rather intimating by his manner that this was just the dirty sort of trick he would have imagined the other would have played.

'Mr Widgeon is the nephew of my old friend, Lord Blicester.'

'Ah?' said Captain Bradbury, hiding with a ham-like hand a yawn that seemed to signify that Freddie's foul antecedents were of little interest to him. It was plain that this was not going to be one of those sudden friendships. Captain Bradbury was obviously feeling that a world fit for heroes to live in should contain the irreducible minimum of Widgeons: while, as for Freddie, the last person he wanted hanging about the place at this highly critical point in his affairs was a richly tanned military man with deep-set eyes and a natty moustache.

However, he quickly rallied from his momentary agitation. Once that volume of Tennyson came, he felt, he would pretty soon put this bird where he belonged. A natty moustache is not everything. Nor is a rich tan. And the same may be said of deep-set eyes. What bungs a fellow over with a refined and poetical girl is Soul. And in the course of the next few days Freddie expected to have soul enough for six. He exerted himself, accordingly, to be the life of the party, and so successful were his efforts that, as they were leaving, Captain Bradbury drew him aside and gave him the sort of look he would have given a Pathan discovered pinching the old regiment's rifles out on the North-Western Frontier. And it was only now that Freddie really began to appreciate the other's physique. He had had no notion that they were making the soldiery so large nowadays.

'Tell me, Pridgeon . . .'

'Widgeon,' said Freddie, to keep the records straight.

'Tell me, Widgeon, are you making a long stay in these parts?'

'Oh, yes. Fairly longish.'

'I shouldn't.'

'You wouldn't?'

'Not if I were you.'

'But I like the scenery.'

'If you got both eyes bunged up, you wouldn't be able to see the scenery.'

'Why should I get both eyes bunged up?'

'You might.'

'But why?'

'I don't know. You just might. These things happen. Well, good evening, Widgeon,' said Captain Bradbury and hopped into his two-seater like a performing elephant alighting on an upturned barrel. And Freddie made his way to the Blue Lion in Tudsleigh village, where he had established his headquarters.

It would be idle to deny that this little chat gave Frederick Widgeon food for thought. He brooded on it over his steak and French fried that night, and was still brooding on it long after he had slid between the sheets and should have been in a restful sleep. And when morning brought its eggs and bacon and coffee he began to brood on it again.

He's a pretty astute sort of chap, Freddie, and he had not failed to sense the threatening note in the Captain's remarks. And he was somewhat dubious as to what to do for the best. You see, it was the first time anything of this sort had happened to him. I suppose, all in all, Freddie Widgeon has been in love at first sight with possibly twenty-seven girls in the course of his career: but hitherto everything had been what you might call plain sailing. I mean, he would flutter round for a few days and then the girl, incensed by some floater on his part or possibly merely unable to stand the sight of him any longer, would throw him out on his left ear, and that would be that. Everything pleasant and agreeable and orderly, as you might say. But this was different.

Here he had come up against a new element, the jealous rival, and it was beginning to look not so good.

It was the sight of Tennyson's poems that turned the scale. The volume had arrived early on the previous day, and already he had mugged up two-thirds of the 'Lady of Shalott'. And the thought that, if he were to oil out now, all this frightful sweat would be so much dead loss, decided the issue. That afternoon he called once more at Tudsleigh Court, prepared to proceed with the matter along the lines originally laid out. And picture his astonishment and delight when he discovered that Captain Bradbury was not among those present.

There are very few advantages about having a military man as a rival in your wooing, but one of these is that every now and then such a military man has to pop up to London to see the blokes at the War Office. This Captain Bradbury had done today, and it was amazing what a difference his absence made. A gay confidence seemed to fill Freddie as he sat there wolfing buttered toast. He had finished the 'Lady of Shalott' that morning and was stuffed to the tonsils with good material. It was only a question of time, he felt, before some chance remark would uncork him and give him the cue to do his stuff.

And presently it came. Lady Carroway, withdrawing to write letters, paused at the door to ask April if she had any message for her Uncle Lancelot.

'Give him my love,' said April, 'and say I hope he likes Bournemouth.'

The door closed. Freddie coughed.

'He's moved then?' he said.

'I beg your pardon?'

'Just a spot of persiflage. Lancelot, you know. Tennyson, you know. You remember in the "Lady of Shalott" Lancelot was putting in most of his time at Camelot.'

The girl stared at him, dropping a slice of bread-and-butter in her emotion.

'You don't mean to say you read Tennyson, Mr Widgeon?'

'Me?' said Freddie. 'Tennyson? Read Tennyson? Me read Tennyson? Well, well, well! Bless my soul! Why, I know him by heart – some of him.'

'So do I! "Break, break, break, on your cold grey stones, oh Sea . . ."'

'Quite. Or take the "Lady of Shalott".'

'"I hold it truth with him who sings . . ."'

'So do I, absolutely. And then, again, there's the "Lady of Shalott". Dashed extraordinary that you should like Tennyson, too.'

'I think he's wonderful.'

'What a lad! That "Lady of Shalott"! Some spin on the ball there.'

'It's so absurd, the way people sneer at him nowadays.'

'The silly bounders. Don't know what's good for them.'

'He's my favourite poet.'

'Mine, too. Any bird who could write the "Lady of

Shalott" gets the cigar or coconut, according to choice, as far as I'm concerned.'

They gazed at one another emotionally.

'Well, I'd never have thought it,' said April.

'Why not?'

'I mean, you gave me the impression of being . . . well, rather the dancing, night-club sort of man.'

'What! Me? Night clubs? Good gosh! Why, my idea of a happy evening is to curl up with Tennyson's latest.'

'Don't you love "Locksley Hall"?'

'Oh, rather. And the "Lady of Shalott".'

'And "Maud"?'

'Aces,' said Freddie. 'And the "Lady of Shalott".'

'How fond you seem of the "Lady of Shalott"!'

'Oh, I am.'

'So am I, of course. The river here always reminds me so much of that poem.'

'Why, of course it does!' said Freddie. 'I've been trying to think all the time why it seemed so dashed familiar. And, talking of the river, I suppose you wouldn't care for a row up it tomorrow?'

The girl looked doubtful.

'Tomorrow?'

'My idea was to hire a boat, sling in a bit of chicken and ham and a Tennyson . . .'

'But I had promised to go to Birmingham tomorrow with Captain Bradbury to help him choose a fishing-rod. Still, I suppose, really, any other day would do for that, wouldn't it?'

'Exactly.'

'We could go later on.'

'Positively,' said Freddie. 'A good deal later on. Much later on. In fact, the best plan would be to leave it quite open. One o'clock tomorrow, then, at the Town Bridge? Right. Fine. Splendid. Topping. I'll be there with my hair in a braid.'

All through the rest of the day Freddie was right in the pink. Walked on air, you might say. But towards nightfall, as he sat in the bar of the Blue Lion, sucking down a whisky and splash and working his way through 'Locksley Hall', a shadow fell athwart the table and, looking up, he perceived Captain Bradbury.

'Good evening, Widgeon,' said Captain Bradbury.

There is only one word, Freddie tells me, to describe the gallant C.'s aspect at this juncture. It was sinister. His eyebrows had met across the top of his nose, his chin was sticking out from ten to fourteen inches, and he stood there flexing the muscles of his arms, making the while a low sound like the rumbling of an only partially extinct volcano. The impression Freddie received was that at any moment molten lava might issue from the man's mouth, and he wasn't absolutely sure that he liked the look of things.

However, he tried to be as bright as possible.

'Ah, Bradbury!' he replied, with a lilting laugh.

Captain Bradbury's right eyebrow had now become so closely entangled with his left that there seemed no hope of ever extricating it without the aid of powerful machinery.

'I understand that you called at Tudsleigh Court today.'

'Oh, rather. We missed you, of course, but, nevertheless, a pleasant time was had by all.'

'So I gathered. Miss Carroway tells me that you have invited her to picnic up the river with you tomorrow.'

'That's right. Up the river. The exact spot.'

'You will, of course, send her a note informing her that you are unable to go, as you have been unexpectedly called back to London.'

'But nobody's called me back to London.'

'Yes, they have. I have.'

Freddie tried to draw himself up. A dashed difficult thing to do, of course, when you're sitting down, and he didn't make much of a job of it.

'I fail to understand you, Bradbury.'

'Let me make it clearer,' said the Captain. 'There is an excellent train in the mornings at twelve-fifteen. You will catch it tomorrow.'

'Oh, yes?'

'I shall call here at one o'clock. If I find that you have not gone, I shall . . . Did I ever happen to mention that I won the Heavyweight Boxing Championship of India last year?'

Freddie swallowed a little thoughtfully.

'You did?'

'Yes.'

Freddie pulled himself together.

'The Amateur Championship?'

'Of course.'

'I used to go in quite a lot for amateur boxing,' said Freddie with a little yawn. 'But I got bored with it. Not enough competition. Too little excitement. So I took on pros. But I found them so extraordinarily brittle that I chucked the whole thing. That was when Bulldog Whacker had to go to hospital for two months after one of our bouts. I collect old china now.'

Brave words, of course, but he watched his visitor depart with emotions that were not too fearfully bright. In fact, he tells me, he actually toyed for a moment with the thought that there might be a lot to be said for that twelve-fifteen train.

It was but a passing weakness. The thought of April Carroway soon strengthened him once more. He had invited her to this picnic, and he intended to keep the tryst even if it meant having to run like a rabbit every time Captain Bradbury hove in sight. After all, he reflected, it was most improbable that a big heavy fellow like that would be able to catch him.

His frame of mind, in short, was precisely that of the old Crusading Widgeons when they heard that the Paynim had been sighted in the offing.

The next day, accordingly, found Freddie seated in a hired row-boat at the landing-stage by the Town Bridge. It was a lovely summer morning with all the fixings, such as blue skies, silver wavelets, birds, bees, gentle breezes and what not. He had stowed the luncheon basket in the stern, and was whiling away the time of waiting by brushing up his 'Lady of Shalott', when a voice spoke from the steps. He looked up and perceived the kid Prudence gazing down at him with her grave, green eyes.

'Oh, hullo,' he said.

'Hullo,' said the child.

Since his entry to Tudsleigh Court, Prudence Carroway had meant little or nothing in Freddie's life. He had seen her around, of course, and had beamed at her in a benevolent sort of way, it being his invariable policy to beam benevolently at all relatives and connections of the adored object, but he had scarcely given her a thought. As always on these occasions, his whole attention had been earmarked for the adored one. So now his attitude was rather that of a bloke who wonders to what he is indebted for the honour of this visit.

'Nice day,' he said, tentatively.

'Yes,' said the kid. 'I came to tell you that April can't come.'

The sun, which had been shining with exceptional brilliance, seemed to Freddie to slip out of sight like a diving duck.

'You don't mean that!'

'Yes, I do.'

'Can't come?'

'No. She told me to tell you she's awfully sorry, but some friends of Mother's have phoned that they are

69

passing through and would like lunch, so she's got to stay on and help cope with them.'

'Oh, gosh!'

'So she wants you to take me instead, and she's going to try to come on afterwards. I told her we would lunch near Griggs's Ferry.'

Something of the inky blackness seemed to Freddie to pass from the sky. It was a jar, of course, but still, if the girl was going to join him later . . . And, as for having this kid along, well, even that had its bright side. He could see that it would be by no means a bad move to play the hearty host to the young blighter. Reports of the lavishness of his hospitality and the suavity of his demeanour would get round to April and might do him quite a bit of good. It is a recognized fact that a lover is never wasting his time when he lushes up the little sister.

'All right,' he said. 'Hop in.'

So the kid hopped, and they shoved off. There wasn't anything much in the nature of intellectual conversation for the first ten minutes or so, because there was a fairish amount of traffic on the river at this point and the kid, who had established herself at the steering apparatus, seemed to have a rather sketchy notion of the procedure. As she explained to Freddie after they had gone about half-way through a passing barge, she always forgot which of the ropes it was that you pulled when you wanted to go to the right. However, the luck of the Widgeons saw them through and eventually they came, still afloat, to the unfrequented upper portions of the stream. Here in some mysterious way the rudder fell off, and after that it was all much easier. And it was at this point that the kid, having no longer anything to occupy herself with, reached out and picked up the book.

'Hullo! Are you reading Tennyson?'

'I was before we started, and I shall doubtless dip into him again later on. You will generally find me having a pop at the bard under advisement when I get a spare five minutes.'

'You don't mean to say you like him?'

'Of course I do. Who doesn't?'

'I don't. April's been making me read him, and I think he's soppy.'

'He is not soppy at all. Dashed beautiful.'

'But don't you think his girls are awful blisters?'

Apart from his old crony, the Lady of Shalott, Freddie had not yet made the acquaintance of any of the women in Tennyson's poems, but he felt very strongly that if they were good enough for April Carroway they were good enough for a green-eyed child with freckles all over her nose, and he said as much, rather severely.

'Tennyson's heroines,' said Freddie, 'are jolly fine specimens of pure, sweet womanhood, so get that into your nut, you soulless kid. If you behaved like a Tennyson heroine, you would be doing well.'

'Which of them?'

'Any of them. Pick 'em where you like. You can't go wrong. How much further to this Ferry place?'

'It's round the next bend.'

It was naturally with something of a pang that Freddie tied the boat up at their destination. Not only was this Griggs's Ferry a lovely spot, it was in addition completely deserted. There was a small house through the trees, but it showed no signs of occupancy. The only living thing for miles around appeared to be an elderly horse which was taking a snack on the river bank. In other words, if only April had been here and the kid hadn't, they would have been alone together with no human eye to intrude upon their sacred solitude. They could have read Tennyson to each other till they were blue in the face, and not a squawk from a soul.

A saddening thought, of course. Still, as the row had given him a nice appetite, he soon dismissed these wistful yearnings and started unpacking the luncheon basket. And at the end of about twenty minutes, during which period nothing had broken the stillness but the sound of champing jaws, he felt that it would not be amiss to chat with his little guest.

'Had enough?' he asked.

'No,' said the kid. 'But there isn't any more.'

'You seem to tuck away your food all right.'

'The girls at school used to call me Teresa the Tapeworm,' said the kid with a touch of pride.

It suddenly struck Freddie as a little odd that with July only half over this child should be at large. The summer holidays, as he remembered it, always used to start round about the first of August.

'Why aren't you at school now?'

'I was bunked last month.'

'Really?' said Freddie, interested. 'They gave you the push, did they? What for?'

'Shooting pigs.'

'Shooting pigs?'

'With a bow and arrow. One pig, that is to say. Percival. He belonged to Miss Maitland, the headmistress. Do you ever pretend to be people in books?'

'Never. And don't stray from the point at issue. I want to get to the bottom of this thing about the pig.'

'I'm not straying from the point at issue. I was playing William Tell.'

'The old apple-knocker, you mean?'

'The man who shot an apple off his son's head. I tried to get one of the girls to put the apple on her head, but she wouldn't, so I went down to the pigsty and put it on Percival's. And the silly goop shook it off and started to eat it just as I was shooting, which spoiled my aim and I got him on the left ear. He was rather vexed about it. So was Miss Maitland. Especially as I was supposed to be in disgrace at the time, because I had set the dormitory on fire the night before.'

Freddie blinked a bit.

'You set the dormitory on fire?'

'Yes.'

'Any special reason, or just a passing whim?'

'I was playing Florence Nightingale.'

'Florence Nightingale?'

'The Lady with the Lamp. I dropped the lamp.'

'Tell me,' said Freddie. 'This Miss Maitland of yours. What colour is her hair?'

'Grey.'

'I thought as much. And now, if you don't mind, switch off the childish prattle for the nonce. I feel a restful sleep creeping over me.'

'My Uncle Joe says that people who sleep after lunch have got fatty degeneration of the heart.'

'Your Uncle Joe is an ass,' said Freddie.

How long it was before Freddie awoke, he could not have said. But when he did the first thing that impressed itself upon him was that the kid was no longer in sight, and this worried him a bit. I mean to say, a child who, on her own showing, plugged pigs with arrows and set fire to dormitories was not a child he was frightfully keen on having roaming about the countryside at a time when he was supposed to be more or less in charge of her. He got up, feeling somewhat perturbed, and started walking about and bellowing her name.

Rather a chump it made him feel, he tells me, because a fellow all by himself on the bank of a river shouting 'Prudence! Prudence!' is apt to give a false impression to any passer-by who may hear him. However, he didn't have to bother about that long, for at this point, happening to glance at the river, he saw her body floating in it.

'Oh, dash it!' said Freddie.

Well, I mean, you couldn't say it was pleasant for him. It put him in what you might call an invidious position. Here he was, supposed to be looking after this kid, and when he got home April Carroway would ask him if he had had a jolly day and he would reply: 'Topping, thanks, except that young Prudence went and got drowned, regretted by all except possibly Miss Maitland.' It wouldn't go well, and he could see it wouldn't go well, so on the chance of a last-minute rescue he dived in. And he was considerably surprised, on arriving at what he had supposed to be a drowning child, to discover that it was merely the outer husk. In other words, what was floating there was not the kid in person but only her frock. And why a frock that had a kid in it should suddenly have become a kidless frock was a problem beyond him.

Another problem, which presented itself as he sloshed ashore once more, was what the dickens he was going to do now. The sun had gone in and a nippy breeze was blowing, and it looked to him as if only a complete change of costume could save him from pneumonia. And as he stood there wondering where this change of costume was to come from he caught sight of that house through the trees.

Now, in normal circs. Freddie would never dream of calling on a bird to whom he had never been introduced and touching him for a suit of clothes. He's scrupulously rigid on points like that and has been known to go smokeless through an entire night at the theatre rather than ask a stranger for a match. But this was a special case. He didn't hesitate. A quick burst across country, and he was at the front door, rapping the knocker and calling 'I say!' And when at the end of about three minutes nobody had appeared he came rather shrewdly to the conclusion that the place must be deserted.

Well, this, of course, fitted in quite neatly with his plans. He much preferred to nip in and help himself rather than explain everything at length to someone who might very easily be one of those goops who are not quick at grasping situations. Observing that the door was not locked, accordingly he pushed in and toddled up the stairs to the bedroom on the first floor.

Everything was fine. There was a cupboard by the bed, and in it an assortment of clothes which left him a wide choice. He fished out a neat creation in checked tweed, located a shirt, a tie, and a sweater in the chest of drawers and, stripping off his wet things, began to dress.

As he did so, he continued to muse on this mystery of the child Prudence. He wondered what Sherlock Holmes would have made of it, or Lord Peter Wimsey, for that matter. The one thing certain was that the moment he was clothed he must buzz out and scour the countryside for her. So with all possible speed he donned the shirt, the tie, and the sweater, and had just put on a pair of roomy but serviceable shoes when his eye, roving aimlessly about the apartment, fell upon a photograph on the mantelpiece.

It represented a young man of powerful physique seated in a chair in flimsy garments. On his face was a rather noble expression, on his lap a massive silver cup, and on his hands boxing-gloves. And in spite of the noble expression he had no difficulty in recognizing the face as that of his formidable acquaintance, Captain Bradbury.

And at this moment, just as he had realized that Fate, after being tolerably rough with him all day, had put the lid on it by leading him into his rival's lair, he heard a sound of footsteps in the garden below. And, leaping to the window, he found his worst fears confirmed. The Captain, looking larger and tougher than ever, was coming up the gravel path to the front door. And that door, Freddie remembered with considerable emotion, he had left open.

Well, Freddie, as you know, has never been the dreamy meditative type. I would describe him as essentially the man of action. And he acted now as never before. He tells me he doubts if a chamois of the Alps, unless at the end of a most intensive spell of training, could have got down those stairs quicker than he did. He says the whole thing rather resembled an effort on the part of one of those Indian fakirs who bung their astral bodies about all over the place, going into thin air in Bombay and reassembling the parts two minutes later in Darjheeling. The result being that he reached the front door just as Captain Bradbury was coming in, and slammed it in his face. A hoarse cry, seeping through the woodwork, caused him to shoot both bolts and prop a small chair against the lower panel.

And he was just congratulating himself on having done all that man could do and handled a difficult situation with energy and tact, when a sort of scrabbling noise to the south-west came to his ears, and he realized with a sickening sinking of the heart what it means to be up against one of these Indian Army strategists, trained from early youth to do the dirty on the lawless tribes of the North-Western Frontier. With consummate military skill, Captain Bradbury, his advance checked at the front door, was trying to outflank him by oozing in through the sitting-room window.

However, most fortunately it happened that whoever washed and brushed up this house had left a mop in the hall. It was a good outsize mop, and Freddie whisked it up in his stride and shot into the sitting-room. He arrived just in time to see a leg coming over the sill. Then a face came into view, and Freddie tells me that the eyes into which he found himself gazing have kept him awake at night ever since.

For an instant, they froze him stiff, like a snake's. Then reason returned to her throne and, recovering himself with a strong effort, he rammed the mop home, sending his adversary base over apex into a bed of nasturtiums. This done, he shut the window and bolted it.

You might have thought that with a pane of glass in between them Captain Bradbury's glare would have lost in volume. This, Freddie tells me, was not the case. As he had now recognized his assailant, it had become considerably more above proof. It scorched Freddie like a death ray.

But the interchange of glances did not last long. These Indian Army men do not look, they act. And it has been well said of them that, while you may sometimes lay them a temporary stymie, you cannot baffle them permanently. The Captain suddenly turned and began to gallop round the corner of the house. It was plainly his intention to resume the attack from another and a less well-guarded quarter. This, I believe, is a common manœuvre on the North-West Frontier. You get your Afghan shading his eyes and looking out over the *maidan*, and then you sneak up the *pahar* behind him and catch him bending.

This decided Freddie. He simply couldn't go on indefinitely, leaping from spot to spot, endeavouring with a mere mop to stem the advance of a foe as resolute as this Bradbury. The time had come for a strategic retreat. Not ten seconds, accordingly, after the other had disappeared, he was wrenching the front door open.

He was taking a risk, of course. There was the possibility that he might be walking into an ambush. But all seemed well. The Captain had apparently genuinely gone round to the back, and Freddie reached the gate with the comfortable feeling that in another couple of seconds he would be out in the open and in a position to leg it away from the danger zone.

All's well that ends well, felt Freddie.

It was at this juncture that he found that he had no trousers on.

I need scarcely enlarge upon the agony of spirit which this discovery caused poor old Freddie. Apart from being the soul of modesty, he is a chap who prides himself on always being well and suitably dressed for both town and country. In a costume which would have excited remark at the Four Arts Ball in Paris, he writhed with shame and embarrassment. And he was just saying: 'This is the end!' when what should he see before him but a two-seater car, which he recognized as the property of his late host.

And in the car was a large rug.

It altered the whole aspect of affairs. From neck to waist, you will recall, Freddie was adequately, if not neatly, clad. The garments which he had borrowed from Captain Bradbury were a good deal too large, but at least they covered the person. In a car with that rug over his lap his outward appearance would be virtually that of the Well-Dressed Man.

He did not hesitate. He had never pinched a car before, but he did it now with all the smoothness of a seasoned professional. Springing into the driving-seat, he tucked the rug about his knees, trod on the self-starter, and was off.

His plans were all neatly shaped. It was his intention to make straight for the Blue Lion. Arrived there, a swift dash would take him through the lobby and up the stairs to his room, where no fewer than seven pairs of trousers awaited his choice. And as the lobby was usually deserted except for the growing boy who cleaned the knives and boots, a lad who could be relied on merely to give a cheery guffaw and then dismiss the matter from his mind, he anticipated no further trouble.

But you never know. You form your schemes and run them over in your mind and you can't see a flaw in them, and then something happens out of a blue sky which dishes them completely. Scarcely had Freddie got half a mile down the road when a girlish figure leaped out of some bushes at the side, waving its arms, and he saw that it was April Carroway.

If you had told Freddie only a few hours before that a time would come when he would not be pleased to see April Carroway, he would have laughed derisively. But it was without pleasure that he looked upon her now. Nor, as he stopped the car and was enabled to make a closer inspection of the girl, did it seem as if she were pleased to see him. Why this should be so he could not imagine, but beyond a question she was not looking chummy. Her face was set, and there was an odd, stony expression in her eyes.

'Oh, hullo!' said Freddie. 'So you got away from your lunch party all right.'

'Yes.'

Freddie braced himself to break the bad news. The

whole subject of the kid Prudence and her mysterious disappearance was one on which he would have preferred not to touch, but obviously it had to be done. I mean, you can't go about the place mislaying girls' sisters and just not mention it. He coughed.

'I say,' he said, 'a rather rummy thing has occurred. Odd, you might call it. With the best intentions in the world, I seem to have lost your sister Prudence.'

'So I gathered. Well, I've found her.'

'Eh?'

At this moment, a disembodied voice suddenly came from inside one of the bushes, causing Freddie to shoot a full two inches out of his seat. He tells me he remembered a similar experience having happened to Moses in the Wilderness, and he wondered if the prophet had taken it as big as he had done.

'I'm in here!'

Freddie gaped. 'Was that Prudence?' he gurgled.

'That was Prudence,' said April coldly.

'But what's she doing there?'

'She is obliged to remain in those bushes, because she has nothing on.'

'Nothing on? No particular engagements, you mean?'

'I mean no clothes. The horse kicked hers into the river.'

Freddie blinked. He could make nothing of this.

'A horse kicked the clothes off her?'

'It didn't kick them off me,' said the voice. 'They

were lying on the bank in a neat bundle. Miss Maitland always taught us to be neat with our clothes. You see, I was playing Lady Godiva, as you advised me to.'

Freddie clutched at his brow. He might have known, he told himself, that the moment he dropped off for a few minutes' refreshing sleep this ghastly kid would be up to something frightful. And he might also have known, he reflected, that she would put the blame on him. He had studied Woman, and he knew that when Woman gets into a tight place her first act is to shovel the blame off on to the nearest male.

'When did I ever advise you to play Lady Godiva?'

'You told me I couldn't go wrong in imitating any of Tennyson's heroines.'

'You appear to have encouraged her and excited her imagination,' said April, giving him a look which, while it was of a different calibre from Captain Bradbury's, was almost as unpleasant to run up against. 'I can't blame the poor child for being carried away.'

Freddie did another spot of brow-clutching. No wooer, he knew, makes any real progress with the girl he loves by encouraging her young sister to ride horses about the countryside in the nude.

'But, dash it . . .'

'Well, we need not go into that now. The point is that she is in those bushes with only a small piece of sacking over her, and is likely to catch cold. Perhaps you will be kind enough to drive her home?'

'Oh, rather. Of course. Certainly.'

'And put that rug over her,' said April Carroway. 'It may save her from a bad chill.'

The world reeled about Freddie. The voice of a donkey braying in a neighbouring meadow seemed like the mocking laughter of demons. The summer breeze was still murmuring through the tree-tops and birds still twittered in the hedgerows, but he did not hear them.

He swallowed a couple of times.

'I'm sorry . . .'

April Carroway was staring at him incredulously. It was as if she could not believe her ears.

'You don't mean to say that you refuse to give up your rug to a child who is sneezing already?'

'I'm sorry . . .'

'Do you realize . . .'

'I'm sorry . . . Cannot relinquish rug . . . Rheumatism . . . Bad . . . In the knee-joints . . . Doctor's orders . . .'

'Mr Widgeon,' said April Carroway imperiously, 'give me that rug immediately!'

An infinite sadness came into Frederick Widgeon's eyes. He gave the girl one long, sorrowful look – a look in which remorse, apology, and a lifelong devotion were nicely blended. Then, without a word, he put the clutch in and drove on, out into the sunset.

Somewhere on the outskirts of Wibbleton-in-the-Vale, when the dusk was falling and the air was fragrant with the evening dew, he managed to sneak a pair of trousers from a scarecrow in a field. Clad in these, he drove to London. He is now living down in the suburbs somewhere, trying to grow a beard in order to foil possible pursuit from Captain Bradbury.

And what he told me to say was that, if anybody cares to have an only slightly soiled copy of the works of Alfred, Lord Tennyson, at a sacrifice price, he is in the market. Not only has he taken an odd dislike to this particular poet, but he had a letter from April Carroway this morning, the contents of which have solidified his conviction that the volume to which I allude is of no further use to owner.

PELHAM GRENVILLE WODEHOUSE (always known as 'Plum') wrote more than ninety novels and some three hundred short stories over 73 years. He is widely recognised as the greatest 20th-century writer of humour in the English language.

Perhaps best known for the escapades of Bertie Wooster and Jeeves, Wodehouse also created the world of Blandings Castle, home to Lord Emsworth and his cherished pig, the Empress of Blandings. His stories include gems concerning the irrepressible and disreputable Ukridge; Psmith, the elegant socialist; the ever-so-slightly-unscrupulous Fifth Earl of Ickenham, better known as Uncle Fred; and those related by Mr Mulliner, the charming raconteur of The Angler's Rest, and the Oldest Member at the Golf Club.

In 1936 he was awarded the Mark Twain Prize for 'having made an outstanding and lasting contribution to the happiness of the world'. He was made a Doctor of Letters by Oxford University in 1939 and in 1975, aged 93, he was knighted by Queen Elizabeth II. He died shortly afterwards, on St Valentine's Day.

'Had P. G. Wodehouse's only contribution to literature been Lord Emsworth and Blandings Castle, his place in history would have been assured. Had he written of none but Mike and Psmith, he would be cherished today as the best and brightest of our comic authors. If Jeeves and Wooster had been his solitary theme, still he would be hailed as The Master. If he had given us only Ukridge, or nothing but the recollections of the Mulliner family, or a pure diet of golfing stories, Wodehouse would nonetheless be considered immortal. That he gave us all those and more – so much more – is our good fortune and a testament to the most industrious, prolific and beneficent author ever to have sat down, scratched his head and banged out a sentence.'   Stephen Fry

We hope you have enjoyed this book. With over ninety novels and around 300 short stories to choose from, you may be wondering which Wodehouse to choose next. It is our pleasure to introduce...

UNCLE FRED

Uncle Dynamite

Meet Frederick Altamount Cornwallis Twistleton, Fifth Earl of Ickenham. Better known as Uncle Fred, an old boy of such a sunny and youthful nature that explosions of sweetness and light detonate all around him.

Cocktail Time

Frederick, Earl of Ickenham, remains young at heart. So his jape of using a catapult to ping the silk top hat off his grumpy half-brother-in-law, is nothing out of the ordinary – but the consequences abound with possibilities.

UKRIDGE

Ukridge

Money makes the world go round for Stanley Featherstonehaugh Ukridge – looking like an animated blob of mustard in his bright yellow raincoat – and when there isn't enough of it, the world just has to spin a bit faster.

MR MULLINER

Meet Mr Mulliner

Sitting in the Angler's Rest, drinking hot scotch and lemon, Mr Mulliner has fabulous stories to tell of the extraordinary behaviour of his far-flung family. This includes Wilfred, whose formula for Buck-U-Uppo enables elephants to face tigers with the necessary nonchalance.

Mr Mulliner Speaking

Holding court in the bar-parlour of the Angler's Rest, Mr Mulliner reveals what happened to The Man Who Gave Up Smoking, what the Something Squishy was that the butler deliv-. ered on a silver salver, and what caused the dreadful Unpleasantness at Bludleigh Court.

MONTY BODKIN

The Luck of the Bodkins

Monty Bodkin, besotted with 'precious dream-rabbit' Gertrude Butterwick, Reggie and Ambrose Tennyson (the latter mistaken for the late Poet Laureate), and Hollywood starlet Lotus Blossom, complete with pet alligator, all embark on a voyage of personal discovery aboard the luxurious liner, S. S. Atlantic.

And Some Other Treats...

What Ho!

Introduced by Stephen Fry, this is a bumper anthology, providing the cream of the crop of Wodehouse's hilarious stories, together with verse, articles and all manner of treasures.

The Heart of a Goof

From his favourite chair on the terrace above the ninth hole, the Oldest Member reveals the stories behind his club's players, from notorious 'golfing giggler' Evangeline to poor, inept Rollo Podmarsh.

The Clicking of Cuthbert

A collection of stories, including that of Cuthbert, golfing ace, hopelessly in love with Adeline, who only cares for rising young writers. But enter a Great Russian Novelist with a strange passion, and Cuthbert's prospects might be looking up . . .

Big Money

Berry Conway, employee of dyspeptic American millionaire Torquil Patterson Frisby, has inherited a large number of shares in the Dream Come True copper mine. Of course they're worthless . . . aren't they?

Hot Water

In the heady atmosphere of a 1930s French chateau, J. Wellington Gedge only wants to return to his life in California, where everything is as it seems . . .

Laughing Gas

Joey Cooley, golden-curled Hollywood child film star, and six-foot-tall boxer Reginald, Earl of Havershot, are both under anaesthetic at the dentist's when their identities are swapped in the fourth dimension.

The Small Bachelor

It's Prohibition America and shy young George Finch is setting out as an artist – without the encumbrance of a shred of talent. Will George triumph over the social snob Mrs Waddington and successfully woo her stepdaughter?

Money for Nothing

Two households, both alike in dignity, in fair Rudge-in-the-Vale, where we lay our scene . . . Will the love of John Carmody and Pat Wyvern survive the bitter feud between their fathers, miserly Lester Carmody and peppery Colonel Wyvern?

Summer Moonshine

Poor Sir Buckstone Abbott owns in Walsingford Hall one of the least attractive stately homes in the country, so when a rich continental princess seems willing to buy it, he's overjoyed. But will the deal be completed?

The Adventures of Sally

When Sally Nicholas inherits some money, her life becomes increasingly complicated; with a needy brother, a handsome fiancé, who is not all he seems, and a naive generosity of spirit, Sally must turn to doting, clueless Ginger Kemp to set things right . . .

Young Men in Spats

Meet the Young Men in Spats – all innocent members of the Drones Club, all hopeless suitors, and all busy betting their sometimes non-existent fortunes on highly improbable outcomes. That is when they're not recovering from driving their sports cars *through* Marble Arch . . .

ALSO AVAILABLE IN THIS SERIES

Featuring

Goodbye to All Cats

Ukridge's Dog College

Ukridge's Accident Syndicate

Featuring

Mulliner's Buck-U-Uppo

The Spot of Art

Strychnine in the Soup

Featuring

The Smile that Wins

Jeeves and the Song of Songs

The Great Sermon Handicap